MONSTER 💀 HIGH™

DIARIES

MONSTER HIGH

DIARIES

LAGOONA BLUE
AND THE BIG SEA
SCARECATION

By Nessi Monstrata

LITTLE, BROWN AND COMPANY

New York   Boston

Little, Brown and Company

Hachette Book Group
1290 Avenue of the Americas, New York, NY 10104
Visit us at lb-kids.com

Little, Brown and Company is a division of Hachette Book Group, Inc. The Little, Brown name and logo are trademarks of Hachette Book Group, Inc.

The publisher is not responsible for websites (or their content) that are not owned by the publisher.

First Edition: February 2016

ISBN 978-0-316-30080-3

10 9 8 7 6 5 4 3 2 1

RRD-C

Printed in the United States of America

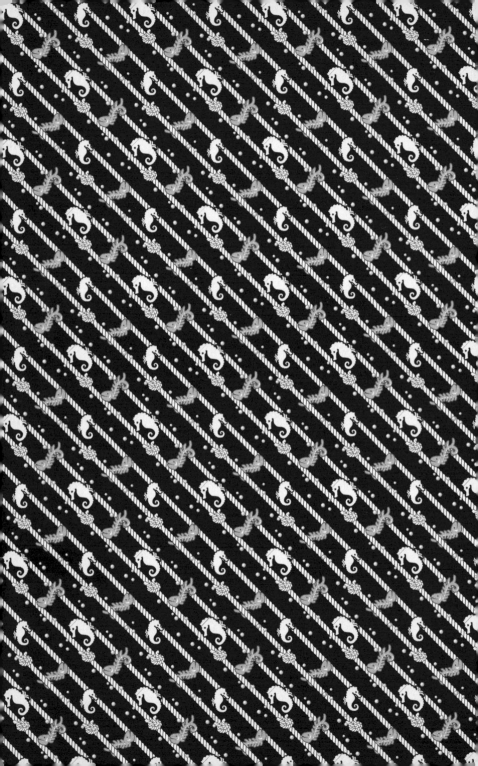

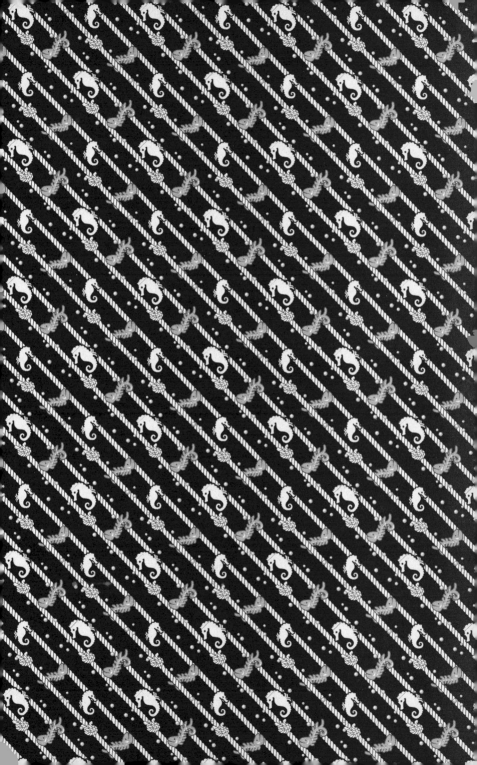

Diary Entry

I am totally stoked for SPRING BREAK! Only
a day left of classes at Monster High and
then it's a whole week of doing nothing except
chilling out on the beach! Sand, sun, surf...
what more could a ghoul ask for? This spring
break is going to be monstrously creeperific.
Kicking back with my mates Down Unda, playing
screech volleyball, teaching Kelpie to surf,
playing in the waves around the Great Scarrier
Reef with the little bros...I am so excited!

Of course I'll miss all my ghouls at
Monster High. It's always hard to be away

from them for more than a few days at a time. And a week without Gil does not flip my fins. But the ghouls and Gil are all doing their own thing this week too, so it's all good! A week to chill out on the beach and kick back in the grotto with the fam while my ghouls and Gil are off having their own amazing scarecations with theirs? Sounds totally fintastic to me!

Now to survive the last day of classes when the waves are already calling to me...

Catch ya Down Unda!

Later, mates,

Lagoona

L agoona!" Gil Webber raised one arm and waved to his girlfriend, Lagoona Blue. "Wait up!"

"What's up, Gil?" Lagoona said, spinning around with a huge smile on her face. She slammed her locker closed and gave her boyfriend a quick hug. Lagoona loosened her hair and shook out the thick braid she'd put in after swim team practice that morning. Her wavy blond hair—sprinkled with faint blue highlights (a side effect of the chlorine in her hair)—curled around her shoulders. She batted her eyes at Gil and teased, "Do you miss me already? Spring break hasn't even started yet, y'know."

"I know, I know," Gil said, laughing as he and Lagoona made their way down the hall toward the Creepateria. The hall was filled with shouting and loud conversations, and some of the guys from the Casketball team were tossing a ball back and forth over everyone's heads. There were only a few hours left of school before spring break started, and everyone at Monster High was restless. Vacation mode was already under way!

Gil grinned at Lagoona and said, "I was just wondering something…." He smiled sheepishly. "Are you *sure* you can't persuade your parents to go somewhere for spring break? Specifically, the resort my family is going to…?" His smile widened. "The Blues would fit right in—the resort even has a saltwater pool. Our families could get to know one another better. Maybe if they spent some relaxing time together, our parents would come to understand one another a little more?"

Lagoona laughed. "Don't tempt me! Your resort sounds like a fintastic place to chill for the week, Gil. But you know my parents can't do anything like that for spring break this year." She shrugged. When you lived in the ocean, just hanging out at home was every bit as awesome as a vacation. "We're hanging at home for the week. Don't forget—I have a beach in my own backyard!" Lagoona nudged him. "Tempt me with your fancy resort all you want, but just know I'll be chilling out, eating on the beach while you order your frosty drinks by the pool. You can think of me when you take your morning swim each day, okay?"

"Of course I will," Gil said sweetly. "It's just that I'm going to miss you, Lagoona."

"I'll miss you too," Lagoona said. For a moment, Lagoona let herself imagine how much fun it would be to join Gil's family on their resort vacation. Ah well, the poor bloke would have to do without her for the week. She knew they would both survive. Still, Lagoona wrapped her arm through Gil's and looked up at him fondly, thinking of how much she would miss him while they were on break.

"Aw, how totes adorable," Draculaura crooned, poking her head between Gil's and Lagoona's. The sweet vampire fell into step beside Lagoona as they all walked into the Creepateria. The three of them joined some of their other friends at their usual table. As she pulled out her fruit salad, Draculaura tilted her head and said, "You two are so scary-cute together."

"Thanks, Draculaura," Lagoona said. She beamed at her boyfriend. Draculaura was right. She and Gil really were a perfect match. If only they could get over the whole freshwater-saltwater issue, their relationship would be smooth sailing! But as it was, their relationship wasn't always the easiest.

Gil's parents didn't really approve of Lagoona or her family. But Gil and Lagoona were happy together, and Lagoona knew that was the most important thing. She dug into her bento box, which was filled with her favorite food—sushi— and between bites continued to chat with Draculaura. "Are you excited for spring break? Any big plans?"

"Oh my ghoul, this week is going to be totes amazing," Draculaura squeaked. She pushed her pink-streaked black hair away from her face and chatted on excitedly. "Father just told me this morning that we are going to be spending the week in *Hauntlywood*! Elissabat is starring in a new movie, and she invited me—*me!*—to be her special guest at the premiere!"

Lagoona beamed at her ghoulfriend. Elissabat was one of the biggest boo-vie stars in Hauntlywood, and she also happened to be one of Draculaura's oldest ghoulfriends. A Hauntlywood getaway would be the perfect trip for the sweet vampire. Draculaura loved any excuse to buy a scary-cute new outfit and get glammed up. "Wow, Draculaura, that's going to be an amazing adventure for you!" Lagoona said.

"I know!" Draculaura said, literally bouncing with excitement. "This weekend, I'm going shopping for dresses with Elissabat and her crew. They're going to help me pick out something to wear to the premiere. Then it will be makeup, and parties, and getting our hair done...." Lagoona smiled and nodded as Draculaura told everyone at the table all about her plans for the week. "Oh! And Clawd is coming along! Can you believe it? My sweetie gets to be my *date* at the premiere."

There were many places where a vampire and werewolf couple couldn't be seen out in public together—Transylvania, for example—but Hauntlywood wasn't one of them. The people in Hauntlywood were open-minded, just like the students and staff at Monster High. Headmistress Bloodgood and the rest of the Monster High faculty were willing to support any friendships and relationships, no matter what a monster's scaritage was. And Lagoona absolutely loved that at Monster High, *everybody's* uniqueness was celebrated!

Draculaura, buzzing with excitement, jumped up from the lunch table and squealed. "There's Clawd now. I just need to run over and let my sweetie know what time we're leaving!"

As Draculaura fluttered away to chat with her boyfriend, Lagoona turned to her friend Clawdeen Wolf—who also happened to be Clawd's sister. "So Clawd's hanging with Draculaura for spring break, yeah? What are your plans for the week, Clawdeen?"

"My sisters and mom and I are visiting my cousins in the mountains," she said. "It's not Hauntlywood, but it should be pretty clawesome.

They live on over a hundred acres of land with tons of space to run. We always have a killer time when we visit them. What about you, Lagoona?"

"Oh, you know—chillin' on the beach. We're not going anywhere special. Just some hang time with the fam." Lagoona shrugged.

"Sounds thrilling," Cleo de Nile said with a yawn. The Egyptian princess wasn't really into kicking back on the beach—unless, of course, she had a waiter and a personal attendant who could help keep her comfortable all day. "I, for one, am looking forward to some serious pampering at the spa. This spa—it's in Boo York—is totally golden, but it's absolutely impossible for most monsters to get into. Very exclusive."

Spas weren't really Lagoona's thing, but she knew that would be Cleo's dream week. So she said, "Crikey, that sounds fancy. I bet you'll have a fintastic time, Cleo."

By the end of lunch, the whole Creepateria was buzzing with discussions of family scarecations and spring break plans. Across the room, Lagoona could hear other groups of friends talking about taking sightseeing trips to Londoom, tours around her beloved Madread, and even more travel to family in far-off places. Some of the Monster Exchange students were talking about going home to visit their parents and siblings for the week. Lagoona could remember how much she had looked forward to her visit home during the Monster Exchange scaremester she had spent in Madread. As happy as they were at Monster High, Lagoona could only imagine how much Kjersti Trollsønn, Batsy Claro, and Isi Dawndancer must be looking forward to seeing their families.

In class after lunch, Lagoona overheard Toralei telling her whole crew about the cruise she was going on. Toralei narrowed her eyes, glanced at

Lagoona, and purred, "All I can say is, there better be plenty of purrfect places for a catnap on this floating hotel. Of course, I'm worried the stink of the ocean won't really help a ghoul get her beauty rest." Lagoona let Toralei's dig on the ocean roll off her fins. Toralei could always find *something* to complain about. The feisty feline was more of a land ghoul, but still, Lagoona couldn't believe she could find things to complain about when she was about to go on a cruise!

As the afternoon wore on, Lagoona began to feel a little jealous of everyone's trips to fun places. Until that morning, she had been seriously stoked about her own beach adventures during a week at home. But after hearing about everyone else's plans, a week Down Unda didn't sound quite as thrilling as it had before. It seemed everyone had somewhere fintastic to go, and home sounded...less special, somehow. The same old, same old. Even though Lagoona wasn't usually the kind of ghoul who felt jealous, she couldn't help being a little envious of everyone else's fancy scarecations!

The rest of the school day flew by in a rush of good-byes and friends' promises to call over break. "I'll bring you one of those fun little drink umbrellas from the resort," Gil promised as he gave her one last hug. "And if you change your mind about joining my family at the resort, I'll save you a seat by the pool!"

Lagoona hugged him again and promised to call him every day. As she wished her ghoulfriends a great week off, Draculaura and Clawdeen both gave her apologetic smiles and told her they were sorry she couldn't join them for their family scarecations. "I'm sure I could sneak you into my trunk," Draculaura offered. "I'll hide you under some of my skirts. My dad and Ramoanah would probably never even notice.…They only have eyes for each other!"

Lagoona knew that Draculaura's dad had recently gotten married, and she was glad to hear the newlyweds were happy. "That's sweet of you, Draculaura," she said with a laugh, and gave her a quick hug, then watched as each of her friends hustled away from the school's big front gates—off to their exciting spring break adventures. As the last of her friends waved and headed away from Monster High, Lagoona sucked in a deep breath. The smell of Creepateria screechza mixed with an odor of damp stones and pine trees. Lagoona wrinkled her nose.

In no time, she would be able to smell nothing but ocean water and salt air for a whole week. The humid seawater breezes relaxed and energized her. She could practically feel the cool waves bobbing her surfboard up and down. The sound of her sister's and brothers' voices always made her feel happy and loved.

Pulling her hair into a loose ponytail, Lagoona vowed not to let a little bit of envy get in the way of her fun. "Forget Londoom and Hauntlywood. Spas, cruises, resorts, and Boo York are *nothing* compared to the beach," Lagoona said to no one in particular, tossing her backpack over one shoulder. With a casual flip of her hair, she set off toward home. "Sun, sand, surf…here I come!"

Diary Entry

Ahhhhhhhh...

There is absolutely nothing better than the smell of fresh ocean air. As much as I love my ghoulfriends, Gil, my mates on swim team, and all the fintastic classes at Monster High, I always feel a little bit like a fish out of water when I'm so far from the beach day after day.

I'm usually a pretty go-with-the-current kind of ghoul, and there's not much that can get under my fins—but I'll be honest about something: I was starting to feel a little bit envious listening to everyone talk about their BIG plans for spring break. I sort of felt like maybe I was the only one without a killer plan.

But now that I can feel the ocean breeze on my neck, squish the sand between my toes, and smell the salty air, my mood is as creeperific as it usually is. I DO have a killer plan! This week at home is going to be totally fintastic. Last week when I talked to Kelpie about what she wanted to do while we're both off school, she asked me to help her with her surfing! It's times like this that being a big sister is so much fun. Kelpie told me she's been trying so hard to get up on her board in the tiny waves close to shore. She's managed to stand up for a few seconds at a time, and then she goes belly up on shore. She's doing great at the baby waves, but the trouble is,

Dad told me poor Kelpie gets nervous and freezes up like a fish stick when she gets out into the deep water.

Kelpie would never admit this to Mom or Dad, but I know what's bothering her—she's worried about coming face-to-fins with the Kraken when she's out in the deeper water alone. Most undersea kids are afraid of the Kraken, so Kelpie has nothing to be embarrassed about, but she still doesn't want anyone to know. I totally get it. I have my own fears too. Facing your biggest fear can be even harder than standing up on a board for the first time. But just like surfing, once you've overcome it, you can't believe there was a time when you were afraid at all. I know she'll get over her fear eventually. And I can't wait to help her get up in some of the monster rollers this week!

Mom told me the triplets have been giggling nonstop about all the pranks they're planning to play on me during spring break. Three little brothers with unlimited time on their fins = major mischief. Maybe if I keep them busy on the beach all day—building sand castles, playing screech volleyball, having barbecues—they'll be so tired at night that they won't have any energy left to torture me.

Now, time to slip into my wardrobe for the week—floppies, baggies, and a tank—and hit the beach. The waves are calling!

Later, mates,

Lagoona

CHAPTER TWO

agoona! Lagoona!" The minute Lagoona got home, three little boys attacked her. Dewey, Squirt, and Tadpole rushed at their sister and flung themselves into her arms. Dewey was soon hanging off her arm, Squirt was wrapped around one of her legs, and Tadpole had somehow managed to get onto her back.

Tadpole clung to her shoulders and screamed, "Giddyup, sea horse, giddyup!"

Lagoona laughed, swinging her brothers

around and around her family's small living room. The triplets screamed with glee, their little legs floating this way and that as Lagoona swam around in circles.

"Goona!" cried Kelpie, swimming into the room. A minute later, Lagoona had yet another sibling attached to her body. Kelpie wrapped her big sister in a hug and looked up into her face. "When are you gonna take me surfing, Goona? When?"

Lagoona shook her brothers off. They went scampering away like a pack of hermit crabs. Once her arms were free, she returned her sister's hug. Then she grinned at all four of her little sibs. "G'day, kiddos. Who's up for a trip to the beach?"

The three little boys all raised their arms in the air and cheered. "I'm going to make the biggest sand castle you've ever seen!" Dewey yelled.

"It's low tide," Tadpole told him. "It's just gonna get washed away when the tide comes in, bro. Let's look for critters in tide pools. Lagoona, you'll play too, right?"

"Of course," Lagoona said, ruffling Tadpole's hair. "Give me a few minutes to say hello to everyone, and then I'll take you over to the beach."

As her brothers rushed off to gather some toys for the beach, Lagoona collapsed on her family's shell sofa. She closed her eyes and listened to the sound of the water coming through the open windows. The sounds and smells of the ocean washed over her, and she sat still for a moment, reveling in how truly creeperific it was to be home. Here Down Unda, chilling in the Great Scarrier Reef and on the beach with the sand between her toes, was the perfect place to spend her week off school. And the quality time she would have with her family was the icing on the creepcake!

"What's up, ghoul?" Lagoona's dad, Wade Blue, flipped into the living room and held out his hand for a fist bump. Lagoona jumped up and gave her dad a big squeeze as Kelpie splashed away. Lagoona and her dad had always been close. Their shared love of catching waves had helped to bond them together when she was still just a tadpole. As Lagoona had gotten older, their bond had grown even stronger. The two of them loved fanging out, just being together. They would go for long swims and talk about life.

"What's up, Dad? You ready for a week of chilling out with me?" Lagoona asked. "I'm going to take the little dudes to the beach to check out the tide pools. I could probably use an assist, if you're up for fanging out?"

"Actually..." her dad said. "Your mother and I have something we need to discuss with you." Lagoona pulled her eyebrows together. It wasn't like her dad to sound so serious. He was usually pretty chill, so when she heard a cautious note in his voice, she couldn't help but worry there was something wrong. "It's about spring break."

"What's up?" she asked, flopping back onto the sofa.

Before he could say anything, Lagoona's mother came into the room. She gave her daughter a welcome-home hug and kiss, then said, "We haven't told your brothers and sister yet, but…"

Lagoona waited. "But…?"

Her parents exchanged a smile. "We have a little surprise for all of you," her mom said. "We decided to stir things up a little bit for spring break this year. I hope you won't mind, but we've—"

Her dad couldn't contain his excitement, so he cut his wife off and boomed, "The Blues are going on a family cruise!"

"We're going on a cruise?" Kelpie screeched. No one had noticed her hiding around a corner, but it seemed she'd been listening in the whole time. "For real?"

"For real," their mom said with a laugh. "We leave in an hour! We wanted to wait until Lagoona was officially on break to share the good news. We didn't want to disrupt your exams. But now each of you needs to pack your bags right away. We board the ship this afternoon."

Lagoona was stunned. Her parents weren't usually big on surprises. Besides, they didn't have a lot of extra money with five kids swimming around. Their vacations were usually focused on spending quality time together near home. Going on a cruise was a big deal. Lagoona couldn't wait to see her brothers' expressions when they found out they would be spending a week on a big cruise ship! They were going to flip their fins!

"Just wait till you see the ship," her dad said to Kelpie. He waved his big hand in the air and looked off into the distance, as though he could already see the ship waiting for them to board.

"There are three saltwater pools, incredible activities for kids all day, endless family hang-out time, and special performances every night."

"There's even a fun talent show!" Lagoona's mom said happily.

Lagoona gulped. She wasn't so big on talent shows, but the rest of it sounded fintastic! Dewey, Squirt, and Tadpole came rushing down the stairs as soon as her dad had finished talking. They each had little buckets draped over one fin, and sand toys clutched under the other. Seeing their beach toys made Lagoona curious about something. "Is there a beach on the ship?"

"Ship?" Dewey asked. "What ship?"

"No, there's not," her mom said, shaking her head. "We'll have to go without the beach for the week. There's also no Monsternet or phone service, so we won't be able to e-mail or call anyone. We can totally disconnect from the world and reconnect as a family."

"What ship?" demanded Squirt.

Lagoona's parents told the triplets about the cruise. The three boys leaped up and down, their buckets and sand toys flying in every direction. "Pack now?" asked Tadpole.

"Pack now, dudes," their dad said, laughing. The boys went off to pack their things. Lagoona could hear them yammering away, talking about playing in the pool and wondering about what kind of activities they would have on board the big cruise ship.

"Are you excited, Goona?" Kelpie asked, snuggling up to her sister. She gazed up into Lagoona's face and smiled, waiting for her sister to say something.

"For sure," Lagoona said, nuzzling her. "It's going to be creeperific! I'm just sorry I can't teach you to surf this week, mate."

"Oh! About that," their dad said, wiggling his fins. "I have good news for all of us! There's a surf pool on board the ship too. You think I'm going to give up a week of catching waves? Not a chance."

"A surf pool?" Lagoona asked. "Really? That's *totally* creeperific. Kelpie will get to practice surfing without worrying about the——"

Kelpie nudged her sister in the gills. "Goona," she hissed. "You promised you wouldn't tell anyone about that."

"Right," Lagoona said, chewing her lip. She had forgotten for a moment that her parents didn't know about Kelpie's fear of the Kraken. She just hoped her sister didn't realize that there was probably a much bigger chance of them bumping into the Kraken swimming around way out in the middle of the ocean while on the cruise than there was near shore by their house. She'd keep that info to herself. Her dad looked at both his girls, curious, and Lagoona grinned back. "What

I meant to say is that this sounds fintastic! A surf pool will be the ideal place for Kelpie to perfect her board skills, eh?"

"No doubt," her dad said. "Now, you two better get packed. Time to make some killer family memories, Blue-style!"

Diary Entry

Whoa, dude. That's all I can say about this creeperific cruise ship. Okay, so *whoa* isn't all I can say, obviously, but it TO-TAL-LY deserves a big time WHOA. This ship is the most glamorous floating hotel this ghoul has ever seen. Seriously. I think even Cleo would be impressed.

From the outside, you can't really tell how fangtastic the ship is—it just looks like a monstrously big boat. But inside, it's all decked out in glittering chandeliers, and there are monsters everywhere who are constantly offering you fresh juice, sushi, and even massages! On top of all that, there are also tons of fancy shops on board. You could live on this ship for a hundred years and never run out of things to do and see and buy.

As soon as we boarded, we went straight to our room to drop off our luggage. Space is kind of tight on cruise ships, but my family is close, so I'm sure we'll be cozy in our two-room suite. We have a couple of cute little portholes that look out over the ocean. It's not quite the same as it is at home—where the ocean is all around us and within reach at every moment, but it will do just fine!

I'm sharing a bed with Kelpie, and the triplets are in these adorable little shell beds that fold down from the wall! During the day, the shell beds get tucked away and look like pieces of art on the wall of our room. But at night, they fold down to become little bunk beds. The boys are stoked.

I haven't checked out the pools yet, but that's up next.

I'm super excited for this family scarecation, BUT...I think I'm going to miss the beach this week. Also, I think it's gonna be rough to look out at the ocean from the dry deck all day long and not be allowed to just jump in and swim along beside the boat. Surrounded by beautiful ocean water that we can look at, but not touch? Crikey.

I'm not going to dwell on those things, though. After all this is a once-in-an-unlifetime kind of scarecation, and the Blue family will make the most of every moment! I could practically live in the pool so I'll just have to do that. And I bet I'll be able to make some new ghoulfriends on board—ghouls from fintastic new places. Meeting new ghouls will help me to not miss my Monster High pals. That's another thing that's great about a scarecation: It's a chance to fang out with totally new people for a week, trying out a whole new you.

Anyway, I can think of a lot worse things in unlife than spending the whole week in the pool with an all-you-can-eat sushi buffet just steps away. A ghoul could get used to this.

Later, mates,

Lagoona

CHAPTER THREE

Miss?" A voice called to Lagoona from above the surface of the pool. She popped her head up out of the crystal-blue water and gazed at one of the most handsome mansters she had ever seen. He smiled at her and asked, "Miss? Can I bring you a cool beverage?"

Lagoona kicked her legs out from the wall, holding on to the pool's edge with her arms. She shook her hair back from her face and smiled.

"That would be great," she said. "Do you have Clamato juice?"

"We can give you whatever you wish," the manster replied, grinning back at her. He pointed over to a large buffet table several feet away. "We just restocked the buffet with fresh sushi, by the way—please help yourself! The rolls are especially to die for," he added with a wink.

Lagoona blushed happily. "Sure, why not?" As the cute waiter strolled away, she thought of Gil. She missed him and wondered what he was doing at that very minute. Probably something very similar to what she was doing—relaxing in a pool, waiting for someone to deliver a cool drink.

Lagoona had checked out the ship's ports of call when they had boarded earlier in the day, searching hopefully for the island where Gil's family was vacationing. She'd noticed they were going very close to the resort where Gil's family would be, but they weren't actually stopping there. She would just have to wave as they sailed past. She wished the captain could reroute the ship just slightly so she could have one afternoon in this oceanside paradise with her boyfriend. But she knew there was no way she could make that happen. After all, there were hundreds of other passengers on board who probably wouldn't appreciate having to take a detour on their scarecations!

"Goona!" Dewey, Squirt, and Tadpole were all screaming at her from the top of the waterslide. "Watch this!" As she watched, the three little tadpoles hurtled onto the waterslide together. A moment later, they zoomed out of the slide in a train of little bodies. They plunged headfirst into the deep, swirling water and tumbled over one another in the pool. All three boys kicked to the surface and popped out of the water, laughing.

"Pretty fintastic, dudes," Lagoona said, giving

them a thumbs-up. "Are you having a monstrously fun time?"

"Are you kidding?" gasped Squirt. "This ship is the *best*! Wanna slide with us?"

"In a little bit," Lagoona promised. "I'm going to grab a snack and get some laps in first." Without another word, the three boys ran to the top of the slide stairs again. The cute waiter returned a moment later to deliver Lagoona's drink. With her drink in hand, Lagoona slipped out of the water and strolled around the edge of the main pool. Just as her parents had promised, there were three pools on deck—one shallow pool for little kids, one big lap pool with a water-volleyball net stretched across the center, and an incredible surf pool at the stern of the ship. There were hundreds of lounge chairs set up around the edge of the pools, perfect for catching some sun between swims.

Lagoona had heard some of the other passengers talking about a dance party they had on board every night. She couldn't wait to check that out. Her Monster High ghoulfriends would love the idea of a dance party in the middle of the ocean! She could just imagine Frankie, Draculaura, and Clawdeen grooving on the dance floor with her. As fun as it was to spend time with her family, she couldn't help but wish she could share this trip with some of her ghoulfriends or Gil. The thought made her even more determined to make some new friends on board. She hadn't seen any other ghouls her age yet, which was kind of disappointing, but she remained hopeful she'd come across some soon. There were a ton of tadpoles on board. Lagoona figured that at least one of them must have an older sibling who was looking to make a new friend too!

Lagoona helped herself to some sushi, making sure to sample one of the rolls the waiter had recommended, and settled into a lounge chair. She let her eyes wander around the deck, taking in all the families and little kids splashing around in the pool, looking for ghouls her age, and...

Wait a minute....

Lagoona pushed her sunglasses up and squinted. "It can't be...."

"Can't be what?" Kelpie said, flopping down beside her sister.

Lagoona stared. There, on the other side of the deck, was an all-too-familiar face. She lowered her sunglasses down over her eyes and shook her head. *Not possible...*"It's nothing," she told Kelpie, hoping she was just seeing things. Maybe her eyes were drying out from too much time out of the water. Yeah, that must be it.

Lagoona took a bite of sushi and listened as her little sister talked about a Hula-Hoop competition the lifeguards were organizing for the pool deck later that evening. "You'll do it with me, won't you, Goona?" Kelpie begged.

"Uh..." Lagoona wasn't so sure. Hula-Hooping

in front of all the other passengers? "I'm not the best Hula-Hooper, kiddo. But I'll watch and cheer you on for sure!"

"Please?" Kelpie begged. "You don't even know anyone here. Why not just give it a try?"

Before she could answer, a familiar voice hissed behind her, "Well, well, well, look what the waves washed up."

Lagoona spun around. So she *hadn't* been seeing things. "Uh, hi, Toralei," she said, forcing a smile. "Wow, what are the odds? So...we're on the same cruise, eh, mate?"

Toralei rolled her eyes. "Looks that way."

"Who's this, Lagoona?" Kelpie asked, grinning up at Toralei. "A friend from Monster High?"

Lagoona and Toralei looked at each other. Toralei narrowed her eyes. After a long, awkward pause, Lagoona said, "Yeah, I guess you could say that. Kelpie, meet Toralei. Toralei, this is my little sister, Kelpie."

Toralei yawned and waved lazily at Kelpie. Then she faked another smile for Lagoona and said, "Well, much as I'm sure you'd love for me to curl up for a long chat, I have places to be and things to do."

Lagoona watched her classmate prance away. She took a deep breath, wondering how she could have gotten so unlucky. Of all the ghouls in the world, why was Toralei the one to end up on her cruise ship? Lagoona was the kind of ghoul who could chill with just about anyone. She loved making new fiends and could always find something in common with most ghouls. But there was something about Toralei's kitty mischief that made it really hard for Lagoona to enjoy spending time with her. She just wasn't very nice, and Lagoona valued kindness over everything.

Now here she was, on a big family scarecation, and it was beginning to look like the only person her own age on board the ship was *Toralei*?

Lagoona couldn't believe this was actually happening. She wished she could call Draculaura or Frankie or Clawdeen to tell them, knowing her ghoulfriends would help her find the fright side of the situation…but with no phone service, that was impossible.

But after a few minutes of fretting about being stuck on a boat with Toralei, Lagoona let her worries drift away. After all, she could just spend her whole day in the pool and avoid Toralei altogether. She knew her classmate hated water, so Lagoona could stake out the pool as her turf and Toralei could stay high and dry, napping on the deck. There was room enough for both of them on this ship. It was all good. "Come on, Kelpie," she said, pulling her sister up. "Let's go play in the pool, eh?"

To try to push all thoughts of Toralei from her mind, Lagoona splashed around in the pool with her sister and brothers. They were having a blast, but every once in a while, Lagoona would look up and catch Toralei smirking at her from her lounge chair on the deck. Briefly, Lagoona wondered if she should invite her classmate to fang out with them—maybe if she killed her with kindness, Toralei would try a little harder to be nice too. Maybe this could be the week Toralei and Lagoona could get to know each other, and then they would become ghoulfriends for life.

Ha! Lagoona had forgotten for a moment that this was *Toralei*. She didn't do nice.

Besides, this was a *family* trip. Lagoona was here to fang out with her sibs, and Toralei surely wouldn't want to do a bunch of little-kid activities. When the boys and Kelpie swam off to play on the waterslide again, Lagoona decided to get in some more laps. It was so relaxing to dig through the water, feeling the smooth pull of the gentle waves, letting her natural swimming instinct take over. But just as she was really getting into her workout, a ball knocked Lagoona on the back of the head. "Crikey!" she gasped, bursting out of the water.

"Oops," Toralei said, covering her whiskers high up in the lifeguard stand.

Lagoona treaded water and looked up at the lifeguard chair, which Toralei was sharing with a scary-cute werewolf lifeguard. Then Lagoona glanced around the pool—it was suddenly full of tadpoles! Her lane was being overrun with little squirts who were all tossing around balls.

The lifeguard howled. "Volleyball time! Clear the pool."

"So sorry, Lagoona," Toralei said, not looking at all sorry. "Looks like you're going to have to take a little break."

Reluctantly, Lagoona climbed out and sat on the edge of the pool. It appeared that Toralei had somehow charmed the lifeguards and persuaded them to organize a water volleyball tournament.

This seemed fishy, since Toralei would never dream of setting a paw in the water herself. So why was she so busy organizing water activities? Had she convinced them to close the pool for volleyball just so Lagoona would be forced to get out? That was just mean.

Toralei looked monstrously amused about the whole situation. For a moment, Lagoona wondered what she could do to get Toralei back for ruining her swim....Then she felt bad for even thinking it. She tried to be nice in every situation, since treating people badly didn't feel good. Plus, it usually came back to bite you in the backside. Lagoona believed firmly that what goes around comes around, and she always tried to treat people the way she liked to be treated herself.

That's when Lagoona realized that the best way to deal with Toralei was to show her that she wasn't at all bothered by her kitty mischief. In fact, Lagoona would join in the volleyball game and have a blast—that would show Toralei how to go with the flow!

Flashing a big smile, Lagoona yelled up to Toralei, "No worries, mate. I love volleyball!" Then she jumped up and dove into the deep end with all the little kids. "Who's got room on their team for me?"

Diary Entry

Ever since I started at Monster High, I've tried to be nice to Toralei. I've made it a point all my life to be nice to everyone, but Toralei's not like any other ghoul I know. She just doesn't want to get to know anyone outside of her little pack of ghoulfriends. In fact, I don't even know much else about her—it seems like the only things I know for sure are that she just doesn't respond to kindness and she's always looking to pick a fight.

It makes me feel sad for her, to tell you the truth. I've often wondered if there's something soft and warm hidden beneath her hard exterior. She's so busy trying to look tough, but I wonder if there's something going on that no one really knows about. Everyone has their secrets—I wonder what Toralei's hiding?

I almost went off the deep end today for a moment there when she shut down the pool for the little volleyball tournament she organized. But then I realized I could have a fintastic time playing volleyball so I just went with it. And you know what? I had a great time! I just hope Toralei figures out a way to have some fun on her own for the rest of the cruise and doesn't try to get in the way of my good time.

It will all work out, especially if I just keep going with the flow.

Later, mates,

Lagoona

CHAPTER FOUR

The next morning, Lagoona woke to the giggling sounds of Dewey, Squirt, and Tadpole leaping from shell bed to shell bed on the wall of their cabin. "Yay! Lagoona's up!" Dewey said, launching himself onto her bed. He held her right eye open and grinned at her. Lagoona tickled him, and he squirmed away.

Squirt squeezed into the space between Lagoona and Kelpie and held open Lagoona's other eye. "Good morning," he said, putting his little nose right up next to hers. She swatted him away, but then Tadpole leaped on top of her and began poking her cheeks.

"Okay, okay," she said, laughing. "I'm up!"

"What are we going to do first today, Lagoona?" Dewey asked. "Huh? Huh?"

Squirt begged, "Will you teach us to surf?"

"All of you?" Lagoona asked with a yawn.

"Please?" the brothers said together. They wore matching grins on their faces. All three were lined up in a row at the end of her bed, holding their hands together in begging poses.

"Me too," Kelpie whispered into her ear.

Lagoona swung her legs out of bed. "Okay, you're on. Get dressed, and we can head out to the pool."

After a quick breakfast—lox and scream cheese on bagels—all five of the Blue kids made their way out to the pool. Things on the main deck were still pretty quiet when they rolled in. It seemed that most people on the cruise ship had chosen to spend their mornings lounging around in the dining room or relaxing on the upper deck drinking coffincinos in the soft glow of the sunrise. But for the Blue kids, the water was the place they went to relax and wake up. It was the perfect way to start their day. And for Lagoona, it was the one place she was least likely to bump into Toralei.

Lagoona wondered what her ghoulfriends and Gil were doing at that very moment and wished, again, that the cruise ship had Monsternet or cell service. She would have loved to be able to call or e-mail Gil and tell him about yesterday's pool volleyball game and the fantastic sushi buffet. And she knew it would have felt great to talk to one of her ghoulfriends about the Toralei situation. Would her friends have agreed that just going with the flow and trying to avoid Toralei whenever possible was the best plan? Since

Lagoona was often the monster other ghouls came to for friendship advice, she knew she ought to be able to figure it out herself. It was just extra complicated, because this was Toralei she was dealing with.

The night before, as she'd drifted to sleep listening to the waves outside their cabin, Lagoona had decided that for the rest of the cruise, she would do everything she could to extend kindness to Toralei whenever she saw her on the ship. Hopefully they wouldn't bump into each other too much—it was, after all, a HUGE ship. But if she saw her classmate lurking around, she would invite her to join in whatever activity she and her siblings were doing. Maybe being extra nice would be enough to keep Toralei from being deliberately mean to her.

Having a plan put a little spring in Lagoona's step, and she was excited to start the day. The previous afternoon, the line to catch waves was really long, and her siblings weren't used to having to wait. Lagoona had stayed off to the side watching, rather than catching waves, to help make the line move faster for her siblings. Every time she had watched the tadpoles line up to catch the little monster-made waves, Lagoona felt a little pang. She missed the beach. Back home, there were waves for everyone—and no one had to wait in line. A ghoul just had to paddle out and chill in the surf, waiting for the right wave to call.

But this morning, the surf pool was empty and waiting for them—like their own private little ocean. Elsewhere on the pool deck, there were a few monsters swimming laps in the salt-water lap pool—including the Blue parents—and a few werewolves enjoying the cool shade of the morning.

Near the pools, the lifeguards were all fanging out together, joking around on deck before the busy part of the day. A few of them came over to watch the Blue kids learn to surf. Lagoona blushed with pride when the cute werewolf lifeguard complimented her on her clawesome surf style.

For the first hour of the surf lesson, Lagoona advised Dewey, Squirt, and Tadpole to focus on getting used to the feel of the board in the water. Though they were eager to hop up on their little feet right away, Lagoona persuaded them to take things slow and practice balancing on their bellies in the surf waves before they jumped onto the boards with both feet. From her own first experience surfing, she knew that learning to feel the rhythm of waves was a big part of getting the hang of it. Before long, the triplets were pros at knowing just when to catch the waves on their bellies, and she had a feeling they would be standing up on the boards in no time.

Because she'd already had some practice surfing in the ocean, Kelpie was able to stand up on her board right away. Watching the way her body moved with the board, Lagoona could tell Kelpie was a natural. If only her sister could overcome her fear of the Kraken, Lagoona was sure Kelpie would love catching some of the monster waves near home.

A couple of hours later, Lagoona flopped out of the pool to stretch out on the dry pool deck to show Dewey and Squirt how to push themselves up to standing on their surfboards. As she began demonstrating the proper form to her brothers, she spotted Toralei out of the corner of her eye. Head held high, Toralei strutted across the pool deck and settled in a comfortable lounge chair.

Lagoona waved and called out to her. "Toralei!" Toralei acted like she hadn't heard her. But Lagoona knew her classmate could hear her perfectly well, since there were still so few people on deck. "I would be happy to teach you to surf..." Lagoona called a bit more loudly, "if you're interested?"

Toralei sneered. "You're not serious?"

"I am, actually." Lagoona forced herself to smile. She hopped up and pointed to her brothers, who had slipped back into the surf pool where they were splashing around in the shallowest part of the waves. "I spent the whole morning teaching my little brothers to surf, and I could show you too. It might be something fun to do...."

For a moment, Lagoona thought she saw the tiniest bit of curiosity and intrigue flicker across Toralei's face. But then it was gone. Slowly, Toralei stood up and made her way toward Lagoona. As she sauntered across the pool deck, she checked to be sure the cute lifeguard's eyes were on her. When she reached the surf pool, she leaned in toward Lagoona and said, "Nothing could drag me into the pool to stand on a slippery, slimy surfboard and look like a fool. I'll leave the child's play to you, Lagoona Blue."

With a toss of her short hair, Toralei spun on her heel and began to strut back across the pool deck again. But just as she passed the edge of the surf pool, Dewey lost his footing on his surfboard and went careening into the air. His board spun, and a huge wall of water flew out of the pool and splashed across the deck. Toralei's platform wedges caught a corner of the puddle, and her foot slipped. As everyone on the pool deck—including the cute lifeguard—watched, Toralei's arms windmilled out. Her legs flew up into the air, and she let out a yowl so loud and so terrifying that even the lap pool swimmers looked up from the water. With a loud *thud*, Toralei landed right on her tail in the middle of the puddle of water.

Sputtering, fur raised, she glared at Lagoona. "You will pay for this," she hissed.

Lagoona raced forward to help her up. "I'm so sorry, Toralei!" She held out her hand, trying to help her classmate up, but Toralei waved her away. "Are you okay? Are you hurt?"

Toralei sprang to her feet, and Lagoona was relieved to see she didn't seem to be injured in any way.

"It was an accident, Toralei. I'm so glad you're not hurt. Dewey, say you're sorry, mate."

"Sorry," Dewey said sadly.

"You planned that," Toralei hissed, her eyes filling with tears.

"No!" Lagoona insisted. "It was just unlucky timing." She wanted to remind Toralei that she was on the pool deck, and water was all around them. But she didn't want to make things worse, so she held her tongue.

"Unlucky for me," Toralei growled. "Lucky for you. I'm stuck looking like a fool in front of every-one. I'm sure you just loved that."

"No way," Lagoona said firmly. "I would never want to hurt or humiliate you on purpose. It really was an accident, and I hope you can forgive us."

Toralei stood up and brushed at the water that was quickly soaking into her fur. "You'll pay for this, Lagoona Blue. No one makes a fool of Toralei without suffering the consequences." Then she stormed off, leaving Lagoona and her siblings staring after her.

Diary Entry

Crikey, Toralei must have been seriously upset about slipping on the deck this morning! She spent the whole afternoon torturing me! I don't know how she has that scary-cute lifeguard wrapped around her claw, but she's somehow managed to swipe control of the pool deck and made it her mission this afternoon to try to ruin my fun.

Right after this morning's slip-sliding fiasco, a school of little tadpoles scampered over to use the surf pool for a rubber ducky race. This crew of kiddos came swooping over to the surf pool and tossed their fleet of rubber ducks into the waves, insisting that they had been sent over—by someone—to have a duck race in the surf pool My sibs and I had to clear the pool while they turned the waves off and cleaned out the pool's filters. There were ducks stuck everywhere! I <u>just know</u> Toralei had something to do with it, since she was glaring at me from her perch up in the lifeguard stand.

Then, right after lunch, the lap pool got shut down less than five minutes into my workout...after all the live lobsters in one of the ship's restaurant's tanks were dumped into the saltwater lap pool I don't know how she managed that one, but I was stuck belly up on the deck while they resolved that issue.

And then, this afternoon, our ship's scheduled stop at a secluded beach—an excursion I was so looking forward to because

I'd give anything to feel sand between my toes—was canceled. I don't know how she managed it, but I'm positive Toralei had something to do with it. She must have overheard me talking with Kelpie about our beach outing and decided that ruining the excursion would be fintastic payback for her embarrassment.

Clearly, she's trying to make this vacation a monstrous fail for me. I'm still trying hard to go with the flow and let the days play out however they're meant to, but it's tough when someone is working so hard to ruin things. I just have to remember the Golden Rule and hope Toralei gets the message soon: Treat others the way you want to be treated.

Eventually she'll warm up. Yeah? Yeah!

Later, mates,

Lagoona

CHAPTER
FIVE

fter their day's adventures by the pool, Lagoona and her siblings were totally worn out and ready to eat. With the surf pool and lap pool closed for most of the afternoon—thanks, most likely, to Toralei's kitty chaos—Lagoona spent the last bit of the afternoon playing on the waterslide with her brothers. When they'd all had enough rides, she bundled her brothers up in a huge, fluffy towel and squeezed the water off their little bodies. As soon as they were dry, all five kids dressed up for dinner and met their parents in the dining room. Lagoona felt like a princess in her new aqua dress with magenta platform sandals. Her hair was long and loose, extra wavy from the sea air, and her skin was sun-kissed from a whole day outside.

"So how's the ship treating everyone?" Lagoona's dad asked, relaxing back into his chair. "Pretty fancy, yeah?"

"It's so fintastic, Dad," Kelpie said. "Today, Lagoona taught us all to surf!"

"Gonna catch some waves out in the deep water with me when we get home, Kelpie?" he asked with a wink.

"Uh…" Kelpie said, glancing at Lagoona for support. "Yeah, maybe."

Lagoona squeezed her sister's hand under the table. She knew Kelpie had enjoyed surfing a whole lot more today, when there was no risk of the Kraken coming to get her. She hoped someday her little sister would get over her fear. "They were all fintastic," Lagoona told her parents. "You've definitely got a school of naturals here, Dad. We can show you some of their great new moves tomorrow."

"About tomorrow," Lagoona's mom said, putting down her chopsticks. "I spoke with the cruise director this morning about the upcoming activities and found out there's a scuba excursion planned for tomorrow morning. Our ship's course will take us right past a beautiful reef, and apparently there are some interesting shipwrecks you can explore. Would any of you be interested in getting off the ship for the day to swim in the ocean?"

"Would I?" Lagoona said brightly. "Count me in! The pools on the cruise ship are totally amazing, of course—and I'm seriously loving the pampering and poolside drinks—but this ghoul would give anything to stretch her fins in a bigger body of water!"

The other Blues laughed. "I take that as a yes?" Lagoona's dad asked.

All five kids nodded eagerly, and they spent much of the rest of the meal planning the next morning's outing. Lagoona couldn't wait! As much as she loved this fancy cruise, she was feeling a bit homesick for the huge, wild expanses of the ocean. And a trip off-ship would *definitely* give her a break from Toralei. There was no way the water-fearing cat would venture off the high decks of the cruise ship!

As Lagoona thought wistfully about the next day's adventure, Kelpie tapped Lagoona's arm and whispered, "Will the Kraken get us?"

"No," Lagoona promised. "The Kraken hides out in the deepest, darkest parts of the ocean, mate.

If we're visiting a reef, you don't have anything to worry about. It's shallow, and there will be tons of beautiful fish around. It's going to be fintastic."

Kelpie's face broke into a relieved smile. "If the Kraken is far away, I'll do it! It sounds fun!"

While the triplets bragged about their surfing skills—exaggerating rather dramatically about their talent for standing up and doing tricks—Kelpie and Lagoona dug into their desserts. The rich, sweet chocolate mousse was a perfect ending to a great day. Lagoona sank back in her chair, letting her eyes drift closed. She was so happy here, chilling with her family, eating great food, surfing…and now a day to explore the ocean. Life couldn't get much better.

"Hello…" a voice purred, and Lagoona's eyes popped open. She spun around, and there was Toralei, looking uncharacteristically sweet. "I hope you're enjoying your dinner."

"We are," said Lagoona's dad, smiling up at Toralei. "Thank you. Are you a new friend of Lagoona's?"

"I'm a...*friend*...of Lagoona's from school," Toralei replied. "Such a funny coincidence that we're on the ship together this week."

"Crikey," said Lagoona's dad. "That is a fun coincidence. Would you care to join us?"

Lagoona cringed. Then she remembered her vow to be kind and welcoming toward Toralei. She pushed out an empty seat and gestured for Toralei to sit down with them.

"Oh, no thank you," Toralei said sweetly. "I was just coming over to say hello and to make sure your family knows about the talent show! Everyone on board has been talking about it nonstop, and I wanted to make sure you all knew about the family competition part of the show."

Lagoona narrowed her eyes. What was Toralei up to now?

"I don't know about the family competition," said Lagoona's mom. "I'd heard about the talent show, but we haven't gotten any of the specifics yet."

"I would give anything to be a part of the show myself," Toralei said, grinning mischievously. Lagoona thought she saw Toralei give her a wink. "But my family isn't into it. But there's a family sing-off in the talent competition. I thought your family would be *purrfect* for it. You could all get up onstage and sing a song together....Wouldn't that just be clawesome?"

Lagoona tried not to glare at Toralei. Getting up in front of all the other ship passengers to *sing*? Crikey. That was her worst nightmare.

"That does sound fun!" Lagoona's dad said, gazing around the table at the rest of the family. The triplets were all bouncing happily in their seats, and Kelpie's eyes were wide at the prospect of a brief shot at fame. "When is it?"

"It's tomorrow night," Toralei said. "You just have to pick a song you're all comfortable singing together, and then you get up onstage and sing it for the rest of the passengers. I'm sure you'd have a much better chance of winning if you put together a little dance routine too. That would give your performance the extra *oomph* to win, don't you think?" She winked at them.

"Can we?" Dewey asked his parents.

"Please?" Tadpole begged.

"We love to sing!" Squirt added.

"Of course we'll do it," Lagoona's dad said.

"Is there a prize for the winner?" Kelpie asked, looking up at Toralei as if she had suddenly turned into the cruise activities director.

"Of course there's a prize. The winning family will get a big shiny trophy and have their photo taken with the captain!"

"That's the best prize ever!" Squirt squealed.

"Oh, one more thing," Toralei said, letting her

gaze linger on Lagoona. "Everyone in the family has to participate. Otherwise, you'll be disqualified." She waved at the Blues, then sauntered off, tossing a casual wave over her shoulder. "Ta-ta."

As the rest of the family chattered excitedly about what song they could sing and what they could do to make their performance extra special, Lagoona felt her good mood float away. She wanted to make her siblings happy, of course, but the thought of getting up onstage to sing was...well, terrifying. While Lagoona loved the thrill of performing on her surfboard or during swim meets in the pool, singing and dancing onstage was a whole other thing. An other thing that was definitely not her thing.

"What's wrong, Lagoona?" Kelpie asked softly, noticing that her sister was quieter than usual.

"Nothing," Lagoona mumbled, picking at the last of her dessert.

"You're going to sing with us, right?" Tadpole asked from across the table. "We want to win!"

Diary Entry

Confession time: I have <u>monstrously bad</u> stage fright. The way Kelpie freezes up like a fish stick when she tries surfing because she's afraid of the Kraken...? Well, the same thing happens to me when I think about performing in front of people on a stage. When it comes to sports, I'm game for anything. But up onstage, singing or dancing in front of people is pretty much my worst frightmare.

I tell Kelpie she's being silly about her fear of the Kraken. But the truth is, my own fear is even sillier...because it hasn't always been this way. I love to dance, and when it's just me—alone in my room or with a few ghoulfriends at a school dance or something—I'm totally up for having fun and shaking my fins. But when all eyes are trained on me, I freeze and go belly up.

I really want to help my sister and brothers win the family singing competition. I know how much fun they—and my parents—would have meeting the captain. But I just don't know if I'm going to be able to do it. I'm trying to go with the flow on the cruise, and I'm doing everything I can to make the most of our family trip, but this might be too much. It's even worse knowing *Toralei* will be in the audience to see me make a fool of myself.

No way, mate. I just don't know if I can do it.

Maybe our scuba excursion today will take so long that they'll have to postpone the talent show....A ghoul can hope, right? Ah well

For now I'll try not to think about the family singing competition. Time to focus on a day in the ocean. This is just what I've been waiting for—a day to chill in the wide-open water. It's going to be FINTASTIC...unless, of course, we bump into the Kraken. (Kidding! Crikey, I hope Kelpie doesn't find out I was even joking about that!)

Later, mates,

Lagoona

CHAPTER SIX

When Lagoona woke the next morning, she felt refreshed from a great night's sleep. She hopped out of bed and peeked out of the portholes. Her hopes for a day in the ocean sank when she saw that the sky was overcast. Big gray clouds hung low in the sky around the cruise ship, and the sea was much choppier than it had been the past few days.

The rest of the family woke up a few minutes after Lagoona, and Wade Blue made his way up to the main deck to find out if their excursion to the reef was still on. Everyone cheered when he returned to the cabin with good news—their day trip hadn't been canceled because of storm clouds on the horizon! They would be splashing around in the ocean in no time.

Lagoona and her family all dressed in their swimsuits quickly, then grabbed a bite to eat from the ship's grab-and-go Creepateria. They gathered with the small crowd of monsters who had congregated near the ship's main exit ramp, waiting to disembark for the excursion. Most of the cruise ship passengers were going to remain on board the ship for the day to relax on deck or play in the pools. Only about a dozen were making the trek out to the reef for snorkeling and scuba diving. Many more had signed up, but with the cloudy skies and choppy seas, some of the less water-savvy passengers had bowed out of the excursion at the last minute. Lagoona was glad her family still wanted to go. She wasn't going to miss this chance to dip her toes in the ocean for anything!

"G'day, ocean explorers!" called a smiling ghoul in a bright green wet suit. "I'm Sandy, and I'll be one of the guides taking you out to the reef today. As you can see, our weather isn't perfect, but we're hoping these storm clouds will blow over and we'll get a bright and beautiful day in the ocean."

The triplets cheered, and the rest of the group couldn't help but smile.

"This is Sam, and he's going to be taking one group of explorers out to the reef this mornin'. I'll be captaining one of our expedition boats today. If you have any questions or concerns while we're out at sea, don't be shy! You can ask me or Sam, and we'll be happy to help ya out."

Lagoona and the rest of the group learned they would be shuttled out to the reef in small motorboats, since their cruise ship was docked out in the middle of the sea. At the end of their day trip, Sam and Sandy would motor them back to the big ship. Dewey, Squirt, and Tadpole were all clamoring to be first in the speedboats—in their enthusiasm to get off the cruise ship for the day, they nearly knocked another passenger overboard.

Lagoona and Kelpie pulled their brothers back and held them close, eager to avoid any accidents. Toralei traipsed by with a towel and a bag full of magazines and sunscreen, and the Blue tadpoles and Kelpie all waved excitedly at her. Toralei flipped her sunglasses down from the top of her head and pretended not to notice.

"Hope you have a great day relaxing, mate," Lagoona called after her. In a light tone, she added, "Lucky for you, there's no risk of getting splashed by any of these three monsters today."

Toralei spun around, her eyes surveying the Blue family gathered together. When she saw that Kelpie's and Lagoona's arms were linked together, her lip curled into a sneer. She cocked her head and said, "Right." With a small smile, she added, "Be careful out there, kids—hopefully no fishermen will catch you in their nets." She lifted her eyebrows, then walked on.

Kelpie scowled at her. "That wasn't very nice. Why would she say something like that, Lagoona?"

"I'm not sure Toralei knows *how* to be nice," Lagoona replied. She smiled at her sister. "But even when people aren't nice, it doesn't mean we should treat them that way. It never hurts to be nice...though sometimes, it's kinda hard."

A few minutes later, the two small motorboats heading out to the reef were loaded up with passengers. The Blue family was riding alone in one of the boats with Sam, who reminded Lagoona a little of Gil. As they zipped through the salty waves toward the reef, Lagoona thought about how much she would like to take Gil on a snorkeling adventure sometime. She would just love to show him some of her favorite fish in the sea—the colors on ocean fish were so much more vivid than the creatures that lived in Gil's fresh-water abode!

"There it is!" Kelpie said, gripping Lagoona's arm and pointing at the sea stretched out in front of their boat. "The reef!"

Sure enough, the water ahead of them was a bright, brilliant teal—a sign that they were approaching shallower water. For most of their cruise, the ocean water around them was emerald green or beautiful navy, depending on how the sun was shining upon it. Today, because of the thick clouds gathering overhead, the sea looked much blacker than it had at any point in their trip so far. But even without the sun, the reef stood out like a bright, sparkling jewel in the middle of the sea. Lagoona couldn't wait to dive in.

As soon as Sam anchored their boat on the far edge of the reef, Dewey, Squirt, and Tadpole launched themselves from the side of the boat and swam off to explore the colorful coral nearby. They were eager to search for treasure—from one of the nearby shipwrecks—that might be hiding in undersea nooks and crannies.

Lagoona waited patiently as Kelpie scanned the horizon for any sign of the Kraken, then she and her sister set off to explore the reef together. Lagoona kicked her fins and glided through the water, relishing the feeling of the ocean water against her skin that she had been missing so much. She and Kelpie swam a couple of quick laps around the perimeter of the reef, and then the two ghouls met up with their parents so they could explore together as a family.

"Should we—" Lagoona's father began to suggest a plan, but his voice was cut off by a long, low rumble of thunder. Far off in the distance, lightning flashed high above the clouds. Lagoona gazed up to the sky and saw that the clouds overhead appeared to be moving—they were gathering and shifting, rumbling and tossing right over the reef. The sky looked alive, and it was obvious to everyone that a storm was rolling in—fast.

"Oy!" Sam called from inside the small motorboat. "Load up, mates. We've got to get back to the ship, fast."

The passengers who had gotten a lift out to the reef with Sandy in the other motorboat returned to their shuttle quickly. None of them had ventured far, so in less than a minute, the other excursion boat was motoring back to the cruise ship. But the Blues, who were all more comfortable in water, had spread out quickly and had farther to swim to get back to the shuttle boat. Sam waved his arms in the air, whistling to get their attention.

Lagoona peered across the reef, searching for her three brothers. Two of the boys—Squirt and Tadpole—were playing on the far side of the reef, caught up in a game of tag with two playful vampire dolphins. Over the rumbling thunder, she could hear their laughter and knew they hadn't heard Sam's warning call. Sam's motorboat couldn't get over the reef to collect them, so Lagoona's parents were already making their way across the reef to fetch them.

Farther away, on the opposite side of the reef, Lagoona spotted Dewey diving for treasure on his own. His little head bobbed up to the surface of the water every minute or so, then he dove back down to explore the reef's buried treasures. "Kelpie," Lagoona said to her sister, "you get in the shuttle boat and wait there with Sam. I'll swim over and collect Dewey while Mom and Dad round up the other two boys."

"No," Kelpie said, her chin jutted out stubbornly. "I'm not letting you go without me."

Lagoona sighed and nodded. She knew Kelpie was afraid of being left alone—especially in the sea during a storm—so she agreed to let her tag along. Thunder cracked in the sky. The storm was closing in on them. They had to hurry. Lagoona swam toward Dewey as quickly as she could, hoping her sister was right behind her. She wanted to wait for Kelpie, but she also knew they had to get everyone out of the open water fast. If the storm hit while they were still out in the middle of the ocean without shelter...Well, she didn't want to think about it. They needed to get back to the cruise ship right away.

When she was only halfway across the reef, Kelpie began to scream—shrill, terrified screams that were almost carried away by the howling wind. Lagoona turned back and saw that her sister was frozen with fear about midway between the shuttle boat and herself. Kelpie's arm was outstretched, and she was pointing toward Dewey in the distance. Lagoona looked, and that's when she saw it: dark, swirling shadows in the water below her brother. Lagoona's stomach clenched with fear.

"Kraken!" Kelpie screamed. "It's the Kraken!"

Lagoona was torn between her brother and her sister. She desperately wanted to go back to her sister, to comfort her—but she knew she had to get to Dewey. They had to get out of open water *now*. Her brother still hadn't noticed the storm had rolled in, and he certainly didn't seem to have noticed that there was some sort of large, dark creature in the water below him as he bobbled up and down. Lagoona swam toward her brother even faster. She knew her sister would be safe in the center of the reef. The Kraken only liked the deepest, darkest parts of the sea. At least, that's what everyone had always said....

When Lagoona came up to check the surface of the water, she noticed her sister's screams had subsided. She turned back to check on her and saw that Kelpie was now swimming—at full-speed—toward Lagoona and Dewey.

"Kelpie," Lagoona called, nearly choking on a wave. "Stop!" But Kelpie didn't stop. Instead, she took powerful strokes through the water, closing in on Dewey and Lagoona. Thunder boomed, and the lightning struck closer.

By the time Lagoona reached her brother, Kelpie had caught up to her. Together, the sisters pulled their brother out of the deep water and pointed across the reef to where their parents and brothers were waiting for them. "Dewey, mate," Lagoona said, trying to keep her voice calm, "we've got to get back to the ship. There's a storm coming."

Dewey shrugged, flipped onto his back, and paddled toward the motorboat. "Okay, thanks, Goona. Race ya, Kelpie!" He grinned, waved, and skimmed across the reef.

Kelpie shivered beside Lagoona as the dark shadows converged in the water below them. Kelpie's face was white with fear. Tears streaked down her wet face, and her voice cracked when she said, "Is he safe now?"

Lagoona took her sister's arm and guided her into the shallow water above the reef. "He's safe," she promised. The waves were really choppy, so it was hard to see anything below the surface without diving deeper to explore. Squinting, Lagoona took one last look toward the shadows under the surface in the deeper water. She couldn't tell what was down there, but there was no time to figure it out. They had to get back to the ship now!

Suddenly, a slippery head popped up out of the water. Then another, and another, and another… Laughing with relief, Lagoona turned Kelpie around and pointed toward the "shadows." "Look! It's a family of friendly jellyfish monsters!" she told her sister. The gray-skinned monsters were slick and friendly looking, and two of them— kids, she guessed—were tumbling playfully in the water together.

Kelpie smiled and wiped her eyes. "So it wasn't the Kraken?"

Lagoona shook her head and smiled. "Not the Kraken."

One of the larger jellyfish monsters kept a close eye on Dewey as he swam toward the motorboat. "Is that little dude with you?" the jellyfish monster asked Lagoona.

"Yeah."

"We spotted him swimming over here all alone and came by to keep an eye on him. Didn't want anything to happen to him with the storm coming."

"Thanks, mate," Lagoona said gratefully. "Appreciate the assist. It's good to know us sea creatures all keep an eye out for one another." She winked, and the family of jellyfish monsters disappeared under the surface again. Relieved, Kelpie and Lagoona paddled back toward the motorboat. Rain had begun to patter down around them. The thunder was growing louder by the minute. Once they were all safely on the boat and Sam had them motoring back toward the ship, Lagoona wrapped her towel around her sister's shoulder and hugged her. She leaned in to ask, "What made you come after me back there, Kelpie? Especially when you thought the Kraken was out there?"

Kelpie rested her head on Lagoona's shoulder, and Lagoona felt her sister shrug. Finally, Kelpie looked up at her. Her jaw was set when she said, "I wasn't going to let the Kraken get my brother."

Lagoona grinned, her body relaxing against her sister's. "You're a great sister, Kelpie. And you're really brave."

Kelpie held her sister's hand tight and said, "You are too, Goona. I learned everything I know about being a sister—and being brave—from you."

Diary Entry

There have been many times when I've wondered how my little sibs get along without me when I'm off at Monster High. My parents are absolutely fintastic, of course, and they take such great care of our family. But still I sometimes wonder what things are like in the Blue house when there are a bunch of little kiddos swimming around without a big sister to keep an extra eye on them.

But after seeing what Kelpie did at the reef today—putting aside her own fear to make sure Dewey was safe—I know that my little bros are in good hands with her when I'm not around. I'm so lucky I have such a loving, supportive family. (And how great was it when that family of jellyfish monsters swam by to keep a lookout on Dewey?! My bigger undersea family is an extra perk of my saltwater scaritage. It's totally spooktacular that so many of the creatures in the sea try to look out for one another. I just love that about the ocean!)

Even though I tried to act chill when Kelpie pointed out the shadows under the water, I've gotta admit I was totally freaked. No one wants to see anyone—especially family!—scared or in danger, and Kelpie was seriously flipping out. I was nervous out there with the storm coming and with those strange dark shadows swimming around my little bro. I don't know what I'd do if something happened to one of my family members. They mean everything to me.

But we're all safe now, chillin' and relaxing after some quality time in the surf—even if that was a shorter swim than I would have liked.

I'm writing this entry from inside our cabin. The captain closed the deck because of the storm. It's going to be a big one, so all the pools on the ship are closed until the sea calms down again. Rockin' and rolling waves don't usually get to me, but that motorboat ride from the reef back to the ship actually was pretty intense. With the waves tossing us to and fro, I was starting to wonder if we'd even make it back. But Sam is a great captain, and he had things under control.

Now that we're back on board and stuck weathering out the storm inside this rolling ship, I can't help but think of how Toralei must be handling all of this. Crikey—we're stuck in the middle of a bouncing ship, with a crazy storm pounding us from all sides. I know Toralei hates water, and there's no way to stay dry in a storm like this in the middle of the ocean. I hope she's handling it okay....

Later, mates,

Lagoona

CHAPTER SEVEN

By late that afternoon, the storm was so intense that the main deck was closed to cruise ship passengers and everyone was ushered into the larger ballrooms belowdecks. The waves and whitecaps were so high that sprays of water were actually crashing up and over the ship's main deck, soaking the floors with water. With each toss of the boat, the swimming pools were emptied, then filled up once again as soon as the next wave hit. The enormous cruise ship was tossed around in the ocean like the fleet of rubber ducks that had been bouncing around in the surf pool the day before.

To try to keep the passengers happy and comfortable, the cruise ship's activities director set up movies and games in the ballrooms. They organized karaoke and created video game stations, and there were hundreds of board and card games for families and groups of friends to choose from. The ship's rocking seemed less noticeable below the water's surface, so the first mate recommended that everyone come out of the above-deck cabins and staterooms to weather the storm in the lower ballrooms. Going on the lower decks helped most of the passengers, but some still really struggled with seasickness and felt miserable no matter *where* they were on board.

Lagoona had lived through a good number of storms and hurricanes during her years in the sea, so the ocean's turbulence didn't really faze her. She and her siblings settled in to play a game of Monsteropoly at a large table in the ship's biggest ballroom. Whenever the ship rolled to the side, the game pieces would shift on the board, which just added to the fun. Every time someone's game piece, coffin, or castle moved across the board because of the storm, Lagoona's family would leave the piece wherever it landed. The triplets decided this way of playing the game was much more exciting than usual!

Though everyone in the family tried to keep a cheery attitude, all the Blues were a little bummed they were forced to remain inside all day. Lagoona had gone through an entire tube of monsterizer in just a few hours—the air below-decks was dry and stuffy, and her skin was drying out quickly without regular dips in the pool. The triplets, who were buzzing with energy, were getting reckless being confined indoors.

They kept insisting that it would be *fun* to swim in the pools while the ship was rocking and rolling. "All the swimming pools are surf pools right now!" Squirt argued. "It's like the real ocean out there!"

"*Pleeeease*, can we sneak out to the pools to practice our surfing in big waves?" Tadpole begged.

"No one will even know we're out there!" Dewey added. "We're the only dudes brave enough to go out on deck." But for the safety of all their passengers, the ship's crew had asked everyone to stay out of the elements, and Lagoona didn't want to break the rules—even for the chance to catch some killer waves. She also didn't want to put her brothers in any danger, and it was obvious this storm brought the potential for danger.

After they finished their game of Monsteropoly, Kelpie suggested that they spend some time figuring out their family performance for the talent show later that night. The activities director had promised that the show would go on, no matter what the weather. So the Blue family tucked away in a corner of the ballroom and tried choreographing moves for the show.

The night before, they had all agreed to perform the Monster High fright song during the talent show. Lagoona had taught her whole family the song the previous summer, and it was the only song all seven of them were close to knowing by heart. "And the best part is, no one else on board will know it!" Kelpie had said happily. "When we sing the Monster High song, all the other monsters on the cruise will find out how great your school is, Goona!"

"Toralei will know it," Lagoona mumbled. She'd been trying to stay upbeat, to hide her anxiety from her parents and her siblings, but she was definitely nervous about the performance that night. She'd hoped she'd feel better about it as it drew closer, but instead the opposite thing was happening: She felt more nervous than ever. The thought of freezing up in front of Kelpie and her family really worried her.

Lagoona took deep breaths and tried to chill. She kept reminding herself that if Kelpie could face her fear of the Kraken, surely she could handle a few minutes in the spotlight. She owed it to her brothers and sister to try.

They had only been practicing their song for a little while when Kelpie leaned over to Lagoona and said, "Hey, Goona...isn't that Toralei over there? She looks sad."

Lagoona followed her sister's gaze. Kelpie was right. Toralei looked not just sad—the ghoul looked like she was freaked out of her fur. She was alone, curled into a ball in the opposite corner of the ballroom. Her eyes darted this way and that every time the ship lurched from side to side.

"Maybe you should go over there to check on her," Kelpie suggested, nudging her sister.

Squirt, who had overheard Kelpie, whispered, "You're supposed to ask friends what's wrong when they look sad. I learned that in school."

Sensing Lagoona's hesitation, Kelpie added, "And you're the one who said we should be nice to people, even if they've been mean to us, right? She hasn't really been much of a friend to you during the cruise, but you told me it never hurts to be nice, even when it's hard."

"That's good advice, Lagoona," her mom said, chiming in. "Remember, a storm brings out the best and worst in every monster. Maybe this storm will soften Toralei a little bit. It looks to me like she could use a friend right now."

Lagoona nodded. "You guys are right. Kelpie, I did say that. And, Squirt, that's a very good thing they're teaching you in school. Mom…I seriously hope you're right."

Kelpie looked thoughtful and whispered to Lagoona, "Do you think Toralei is afraid of the Kraken? I can come with you and tell her she doesn't need to worry. If you want."

Lagoona laughed. "I don't think Toralei even *knows* about the Kraken," she whispered back. With her siblings' advice ringing in her ears, Lagoona made her way across the room toward Toralei. She didn't want to see anyone feeling sad or scared if there was something she could do about it. "Hey, Toralei," she said, sitting down beside her classmate. "You okay, mate?"

Toralei glared at her. "Fine."

She was clearly not fine, but Lagoona didn't say that. "I've lived in the ocean my whole life,"

Lagoona said. "Storms can be really scary. But here's the thing you have to remember: They always pass. It's tough to go through it, but there's always sunshine hiding on the other side of the cloud. This storm will definitely pass too."

Toralei rolled her eyes.

Lagoona pretended not to notice. "I can still remember one of the scariest storms I've ever been in. I was a teeny tadpole, and I'd never seen anything like it before. The whole sea was churning, and there was nothing but gray and black—everywhere. You couldn't even see your own fins in front of your face." Out of the corner of her eye, Lagoona could see that Toralei was looking back at her with huge eyes. Lagoona went on, "My mom sang to me through the whole storm, and it was the perfect distraction. Sometimes you've just got to get your mind off your fears—you know, distract yourself—and it helps make the time pass."

Toralei narrowed her eyes, wondering if Lagoona was going to say something else, something to scare her or make her feel worse. After a long pause, she realized that Lagoona really was just trying to help. "I hate water," she whispered miserably.

Lagoona laughed, then covered her mouth. "Sorry, mate, but that's obvious. You're a werecat—the sea's not really your thing, is it?"

Toralei's mouth twitched into a small smile. "I've never spent much time near the ocean. I came on this cruise with my parents so I could stretch out in the sun and take catnaps. But now it sort of...well, it feels like something's going to happen to the ship and we'll all be forced to swim to shore or something."

Lagoona shook her head, looking right into Toralei's bright green eyes. "No way! The ship was built to handle waves like this," she promised. "Nothing's gonna happen. Trust me. We've just got to chill and get through it, and then the rest of the trip will be smooth sailing." Lagoona pushed herself up and held out a hand to help Toralei off the floor. "Come with me, mate. My family could use some help practicing the Monster High fright song. That's what my little sibs want to sing in the talent show tonight." She tilted her head. "Whaddya say? It will be a great distraction."

Reluctantly, Toralei took Lagoona's hand. "Are you sure?"

"Absolutely," Lagoona said, pulling her up. "We'll help keep your mind off the storm. Besides, my brothers could use a few pointers. Their dance moves make them look like fish out of water! They've had enough instruction from me in the surf pool this week—maybe you can help them with their dancing?"

Toralei laughed. "Thanks, Lagoona. I really appreciate this."

"No biggie," Lagoona told her.

Toralei put her hand on Lagoona's arm, stopping her before they reached the rest of the Blue family. "I'm sorry I've been a little...well, mean to you this week."

"I'm over it, mate." Lagoona smiled—and as soon as she said it, she realized she meant it.

Diary Entry

It was really cool getting to chill with Toralei for a while today! My mom was right—the storm did bring out a new side of her. While we waited for the bad weather to pass, she seemed like a totally different ghoul than the Toralei we usually see at school.

She told me that she's sometimes a little rough around the claws with people she doesn't know that well. I hope she'll consider me a ghoulfriend from now on—it would be nice to stay on Toralei's softer side back at Monster High. But something tells me that when we're back at Monster High, Toralei and her pack will be back to their usual kitty mischief.

I'm sure Toralei would never admit to anyone that I helped her weather a storm during spring break, but that's okay. Me helping her out today can be our little secret....I'm just glad I could be a good friend to her when she went off the deep end.

Oh, and the talent show prep definitely proved to be the perfect distraction from the storm! Toralei is a really good dancer, and she helped my family put together this scary-cute routine that's sure to help us win the family song competition. My mom and dad have actually really gotten into the whole performance too—I'm the only one who's been mostly lurking in the background, helping my brothers figure out all the steps and stuff. I think Toralei has noticed that I'm not really doing much dancing myself. But she doesn't seem to mind taking center stage.

Uh-oh, gotta go....The show's about to start. Gulp!

Fins crossed.

Later, mates,

Lagoona

CHAPTER EIGHT

D ewey, Squirt, Tadpole!" Toralei hissed. "Get back here! Your family is on in five!"

While the Blues waited for their turn to take the stage, the triplets chased one another around. In their usual flurry of activity, the boys kept knocking over props and costume racks backstage. They were zipping and dashing all over the place, focusing on everything *but* their performance—and it was clearly driving Toralei crazy. She raked a paw through her sleek hair.

"Ugh," Toralei groaned. "Keeping these three under control is like herding kittens."

"They're full of energy, that's for sure," Lagoona said, laughing as she watched Toralei trying to assemble her brothers backstage.

Toralei kept trying to get the boys to focus long enough that they could practice their routine one more time. "I want everything to be purrfect!" she announced as Dewey, Squirt, and Tadpole scattered in all directions. "Focus, boys!"

Throughout the afternoon, Lagoona had begun to realize Toralei was the kind of ghoul who liked to have things under control at all times. Her take-charge vibe was very different from the chill, laid-back nature of the Blue family—but it proved to be helpful when it came time for them to actually buckle down and practice. Lagoona wondered if Toralei's need for control was part of what made her so mischievous—maybe manipulating people with pranks made her feel like she had a claw up on everyone around her.

Lagoona watched her brothers scrambling around backstage. She kicked back and told Toralei, "You don't have to stick around, y'know. Now that the storm's over and our performance is ready, you're free to jet. We appreciate your help—and we never would have pulled it off without you—but the whole point was to distract you from the storm. Now that the skies are clear again, I'm sure you have plenty of other things you'd rather be doing than fanging out backstage with my crazy family."

"A nap would be clawesome right about now." Toralei yawned. "But I wouldn't miss the Blue family's performance for the world." She shrugged. "I kind of feel like I'm part of the show now. After all, I did whip these boys into shape." She paused, then looked at Lagoona suspiciously. "Are you sure *you're* ready to perform, Lagoona? You've been so busy helping the rest of your family nail their performances, you haven't had a chance to practice for the show yourself."

Lagoona felt a blush creep up her cheeks. "Oh, I'll be fine," she said with a casual flip of her fins. But in fact, she was more nervous than ever. Because Lagoona knew she wasn't the least bit ready for their talent show performance. She had been carefully avoiding dancing and singing in front of Toralei all day. Now it was almost time for the family to step out onstage and she didn't have the faintest idea how she was going to get through it. Everyone else had practiced together a dozen times, but Lagoona had really only watched. Trying to sound chill, Lagoona muttered, "I figure I can just wing it when we get up onstage."

"Wing it?!" Toralei shrieked. "But you'll ruin the performance for the rest of your family! They've been practicing all afternoon. If you get up onstage without rehearsing even the littlest bit, you'll look like a blob fish."

"Wow," Lagoona said. "Thanks for the vote of confidence."

Toralei drummed her long claws together, thinking. Then she looked up with a bright smile and said, "Here's an idea: I don't want to steal your thunder or anything...." She trailed off, then said, "Well, maybe I do want to steal your thunder." Toralei grinned mischievously. "So how about this—maybe I should take your place in the show?"

Lagoona gaped at her. "Like, *you* would join my family in the family song contest?"

"I know it's a little...unconventional," Toralei said with a wink. "But I *was* the one who taught them all the choreography. I know the routine and the song and you...well, you *don't*. Maybe you could just float around in the wings and give your brothers cues if any of them forgets what comes next?"

"Oh, uh…" Lagoona said, brightening. This was a brilliant idea! Toralei could get the attention she wanted, and Lagoona could avoid it. "Do you actually *want* to sing onstage with my family?"

"Absolutely," Toralei beamed. "There's no way they would lose with me up onstage. I'm a natural performer. *Me-ow*!"

Lagoona giggled and said, "Then be my guest. I would be more than happy to let you take my place. Talent shows aren't really my thing." Eventually, Lagoona knew, she would have to face her fear of performing…but thanks to Toralei, it looked like today wasn't that day. Then Lagoona remembered something. "Didn't you say the whole family has to participate, or we'll be disqualified?"

Toralei shrugged. "That was a little fib. You should have seen the look on your face when I told you you'd have to get up onstage to perform a song with your family! *Purr*fectly priceless."

The two ghouls laughed together, and Lagoona wondered if, perhaps, Toralei had a hunch about her stage fright. Maybe Toralei was stepping in to help Lagoona get through a scary situation, the same way she had helped Toralei get through the storm? Lagoona could never be sure, but she had a feeling there was something soft hidden beneath Toralei's prickly fur.

A few minutes later, the Blues—and Toralei— were called up onstage. When they were crowned the winners of the family song contest at the end of the show, Lagoona cheered louder than anyone. And when they posed with the captain for their photo, Toralei and Lagoona joined them for the picture. Lagoona figured it might be the only time Toralei would ever choose to be in a picture with her, but she would enjoy it while it lasted.

That night, as Lagoona and her family made their way back to their cabin carrying their big

Diary Entry

This morning, I got the best surprise ever...
and I think Toralei might have had something
to do with it! Apparently, the storm blew our
ship off course yesterday, so the captain had
to reroute us to a different port of call to
check the ship for damage from the storm.

And guess what? We got to stop on the
island where Gil is staying with his family! It
was so fintastic getting to see him...even if it
was only for an hour.

I spotted Toralei chatting with the captain
during dinner last night—and I think she might

have said something to him about stopping
here! When I asked her if she'd suggested we
sail this way, she smirked and said, "Now why
would I do that?"

I know Toralei tries to make everyone think
she's this tough ghoul but now I know the
truth: She can be a sweetheart when she
wants to be.

Who knows...maybe we're becoming friends.
Or maybe this week together at sea was only
a brief calm before an even bigger storm. I
guess only time will tell! But for now, I'm
ready to kick back, hit the pool and enjoy the
rest of this cruise. Surf's up!

Later, mates,

Lagoona

Start your own fangtastic diary, just like Lagoona! On the following pages, write about your own creepy-cool thoughts, hopes, or screams...whatever you want! These pages are for your eyes only! (Unless you want to share what you write with your ghoulfriends!)

MONSTER HIGH

Monster High

Did you 🖤 reading Lagoona´s diary?
Then you will also love reading
CLAWDEEN WOLF'S DIARY...
COMING SOON!